ONE MURDEROUS WEEK

NANDY EKLE

Cover design by Carpe Diem Publishers

Print ISBN: 978-0-9836691-3-5

eBook ISBN: 978-0-9836691-4-2

To my Husband, Batman

CONTENTS

1. SUNDAY: MY SWEET PRINCE

The sun blares louder than any alarm clock could ever scream. My eyes pop open and look at the hateful light coming in through the window. I will have to get out of bed, but my body aches. I've got a few new bruises, some on my skin, some down deep inside. I wince as my abs contract sending a message to my brain which cries in protest. We must have had a hell of a fight last night. My head sends messages to my stomach to empty out if I made one quick move.

Rolling slowly over to the edge of the bed, I'm careful not to move too fast. All I remember is a horrible fight—I think something to do with my books and a bookmarker. My memory is fuzzy as the pain in my head threatens to unlock all kinds of doors I do not want opened.

I don't remember going to bed naked, but I certainly woke up that way. Looking down at my legs, I see the giant bruise on my left thigh opening up like a flower. Yeah, once my head clears, that spot's really going to hurt. My stiff hands close in fists, and a sharp dry pain races up to join the fire in my head. There's a deep gash in the palm of my hand. What the hell happened there? Maybe it'll come back to me after my shower.

I don't want to wake Mark, so I slide out of bed as gently as I can. If we had the fight my body told me we had, he'll probably sleep a little while longer, but I don't want to take any chances. I deserve some peace and quiet to read my new book.

I love to read. I love opening a book and getting lost in someone else's life, their surroundings, their problems, and forgetting mine. I used to tell Mark that I wasn't only reading a book; I was visiting another world for a little while. He just can't understand that. He cannot open a book and decipher letters and words into a story that fills his soul with feeling and emotion. He just doesn't get it. Makes me wonder if that's why he gets so furious with me all the time, because I have relationships with the people in my books.

After a quiet tiptoe to the bathroom, I pee and start the shower running. I still have no idea what time of day it is, but I can't stand staying in that bed a minute longer.

When I glance in the mirror, I see the new bruise covering my eye. No way to hide that, or the one that decorates my jaw. I decide to stay home from work because I don't want to come up with another explanation. The people who come into the Quick Stop convenience store stare at me every time I come to work with a new bruise. I know what they're thinking; I see it in their eyes. "He must beat her. She must be a retard for not leaving him. Why does a girl stay around and take that kind of abuse?" I wonder that myself every morning when I wake up feeling like I've been through a meat grinder.

As I stand in front of the mirror I look at my belly. There's no mark, but that doesn't mean I don't feel the soft and gushy spot where his fist tried to punch a hole. No, that's definitely sore. My boobs have marks where he grabbed them. He usually wants to have sex after punching me in the eye and then the stomach. By that time I'm so tired and hurt that I let him do whatever the hell he wants just so he'll pass out. God, I must be the dumbest girl in the world.

The air in the bathroom turns warm and humid as the water heats up in the tub, but I continue to stare at myself in the mirror. My scalp aches in a patch on the side of my head, and I discover a lump there. Don't know where that came from, but I will remember to brush my hair carefully. I also realize that my hair is a little damp but not bloody. Well, maybe I took a shower last night after he passed out.

Stepping under the water I feel it sting my skin like millions of tiny little needles trying to perform acupuncture on my arms and legs, belly and face. Ah, the energizing feeling of steaming hot water piercing through me. It won't wash the bruises away very fast, but it will certainly wash away some of the fuzz in my head. I have until noon to call Lance at the store and tell him I'm not coming in, so I intend to take my time and just feel the water blister me.

I stand there in the shower thinking about what had attracted me to Mark in the first place. He's not like my fairy tale prince at all, like I'd always dreamed.

In my fantasy I travel somewhere—anywhere—and a tall, beefy man with a very broad chest, dark hair and dark eyes, and sexy accent comes up to me and introduces himself as a prince. His scent excites my awareness and I feel my face grow warm. He looks at me and takes my hand, tells me he has been looking for me all his life and then sweetly and gently kisses my hand sending thrills through me like shimmers that play havoc with my senses. He calls me and we go out for dinner and dancing a few times, then he gets down on one knee and proposes to me right out in public—just like in the storybooks. My heart trembles and my breath speeds up just thinking about it.

The way I met Mark doesn't even come close to that. I had gone to the Empty Stable Bar with Susan. We were drinking beers, laughing, cutting up. Mark danced up with his bowlegged swagger, very cute but tough, so self-confident.

He wore his jeans tight in the right places, just enough to look interesting. The top two buttons of his shirt hung opened and a little of that beautiful curly hair popped out and waved at me. He even wore those fabulous pointy-toed boots. I remember thinking that just looking at him made me shiver with excitement—of course, I had had several beers.

He step-ball-changed right up to me and smiled that lopsided smile, very square-jawed, and politely asked if he could buy me a drink. We danced and partied until the bar closed, then he came home with me. We made love in a drunken stupor and slept like rocks the rest of the night.

We've been together for a year. During that year, we've had more fights than I can count, but making up is filled with storybook passion. I wonder if that's why I let him stay, just waiting for him to apologize, bring me flowers and little gifts, and kiss me like he thinks I'm a princess. I think I love that about him more than anything—making up.

I get out of the shower, wrap a towel around my head, and dry off. The headache's dulling down a little, no longer threatening to turn my stomach inside out, and some of the achiness is easing up. I tiptoe back into the bedroom to find a shirt, a pair of sweatpants and socks from the cleanest pile of clothes lying on the floor. Mark hasn't budged an inch on the bed so I quickly leave and head into the kitchen.

The door of the cabinet where I keep my meds and Band-aids, stuff like that, gapes open because we never close the doors when we get something—just open the door, find what we need, and walk off. Sometimes I get fed up with it and close them all, but then the house looks weird with all the cabinets closed and drawers pushed in—it's just not normal.

Finding the Tylenol, I take what the label suggests as a good dose and swallow them; I don't even need water. In fact, I nearly crush them with my teeth just to see if I can taste the bitterness, but I decide to swallow them with what little spit I can work up.

Looking at the dishes piled in the sink I remember that we fought about the dirty dishes. He was tired of living in a mess. I told him he could leave, that this mess, this old trailer house, no matter how broken down it is, how full of junk, it's mine—my only possession other than my books—left to me by my grandfather when he passed from this world to the next. Then Mark grabbed my hair.

There's not much to eat in the pantry besides a half a loaf of bread, so I take a piece of that and check inside the refrigerator. Only some beers and something green and fuzzy in a bowl with no lid. There's some store-bought food on the table, but it doesn't look very appetizing, so I take a beer. The clock on the wall says 10:17.

Good, I have a few minutes to read my book. I huddle on the couch discovering new aches and pains.

My favorite books to read are romances. I love the way a woman and a man meet and the chemistry immediately splatters across the pages. I can tell who will wind up with whom before page ten and it thrills me to find out when I'm right. The men are so strong and sexy, and the women are smart and beautiful. They have their arguments, but they always find their love by the end, sometimes sooner. And those erotic sex scenes can nearly bring me to climax just from reading them. Beautiful places, beautiful people, and beautiful fairy tale endings—my heart always feels full after reading a delicious love story.

About thirty minutes of quiet go by. By this time, my sore spots have started to settle back into stiffness, enjoying the idleness of sitting still. But I still need to call my boss and tell him I'm staying home. The clock says 10:47 and that will give him plenty of time to call someone to take my place at the cash register. I get the phone from my purse, which sits in a sprawled position on the kitchen table next to the store-bought fried chicken and potato salad we didn't eat.

Walking out onto the back porch, I dial the number to the Quick Stop and got Lance's voice.

"Hey, Lance, this is Tish. I don't think I can come to work today. I'm pretty sick."

"Well, this is the second time this week. Have you been to a doctor?"

"No, it's just a virus bug going around. I'll be in tomorrow."

"I hope so. I would hate to have to replace you."

"No, you won't. It's just a touch of flu. Twenty-four hours. I'll be back tomorrow."

"Okay. Take care of yourself."

Do I hear pity in his voice? Does he know? Does he know that Mark beat me stupid again? Does he know I really hate that job anyway? That I hate the way people come in there and stare at me like I'm a moron or a freak for staying with a guy who shows his love with his fists? I hate the ones who look at me as if I don't have any brains in my head. I hate the ones who sniff at me like I have the plague.

And then there are the truck drivers who come in and act like they can smell danger and violence on me. They have such stupid little things to say, and then laugh as they leave the store like they're the cleverest men in the world.

What I didn't tell Lance was that I want to take the shotgun from under the cash register and blow all his customers to bits. It would make me laugh to see trucker guts and holier-than-thou guts and my-shit-doesn't-smell guts drip from the walls of his stupid little store.

I walk back in the house, put my phone on the table next to my end of the couch, and curl back into the seat. Still no sign of life from the bedroom, so I open my book to the page held by a crummy little toothpick.

I love those colorful little bookmarkers you can buy at the bookstore, the ones with clever little sayings about time spent in a book or the benefits of reading. I bought one like that, but Mark tore it up. He says all I need is a scrap of paper or a paperclip or a rubber band—just something to stick between the pages so I'll remember where I left off reading. He says I could just fold the corner down for all he cares. He doesn't understand that folding the corner down is cruel punishment to the book.

Another twenty minutes go by. The story is lovely. *Combustible Chemistry* is about a young woman desperately in love with a brilliant scientist, who also happens to be very handsome, but their love is stalemated because he is desperately tied to his job. She wants to find a way to get his attention back on her, but his research keeps getting in the way.

I put my toothpick back in the spot and go to the bedroom door to look in on Mark. He still hasn't moved. He must have been pretty tired after the beating, even for him. Mark is the kind of man who can change gears instantly. One minute he's buying me drinks, slapping my ass and laughing with lust in his voice, the next minute he's ripping my hair out and slapping my face, ramming the pointed toe of his boot into my ribs. And then he's kissing me and telling me how sorry he is, that I'm the best thing he's ever had and he'll never hurt me again.

He's so physical. I think this is what usually makes him such a light sleeper. He's usually the one that wakes me up. He jumps out of bed, and the covers go with him. Sometimes he even yells, "Tisha, get up! Let's find some food! Good God, girl, the day is nearly gone!" And I get up when he does that and go into the kitchen to look for cereal and milk and a clean bowl to feed my man.

I stand at the door and watch him for a minute, emotion flooding my brain. He's on his stomach, the covers across his butt, his bare back facing the ceiling. I can see his dark hair all tousled, like one of the characters in my book.

A prickle starts in the middle of my chest. All that curly hair. I love running my hand through it, twisting it around my fingers and watching it bounce back in place. He's got the most beautiful hair in the world. There's been lots of times in the middle of the night I sit up and watch him sleep with his curly dark hair all fanned out on the pillow.

Thinking about how beautiful he is, I suddenly want to be beside him. I want to rub my hands through his chest hair and feel the tightness of his chest muscles. I want to tell him that I forgive him. I know I'm a stupid bitch and I don't deserve him. I'll do better; I'll clean up the house, wash the clothes. I'll even fold them and put them away. I just don't want him to be mad at me anymore.

I climb up on the bed and reach over to him.

"Mark?" He doesn't answer. "Mark?"

I'm close enough now to see some of the covers around him. My sheets are black, but the black looks even darker. I feel the bread in my stomach try to crawl back out.

"Mark? Are you okay? Mark, wake up!" I hear a little

hiccup in my voice, but I can't help it. "Mark! Mark! Wake up!"

I roll him over and see the blood covering his belly and the holes in his chest.

The last of the fog evaporates from my head and I see the events that happened the night before.

Yesterday was payday, and I cashed my check, which was shorter than normal because I had been off work for a day or two after a previous fight. I went to the store to get fried chicken for supper. I walked by the book section and, of course, I had to stop. I felt the old tug, the need for a new world, a new set of friends and sighs. I was two chapters away from finishing *The Kiss That Never Was,* and I didn't have anything new waiting for me. I do re-read my books when I have to, but sometimes something new is the best prescription ever. I walked along the shelves, touching as many book friends as I could and waiting for a response. Finally, *Combustible Chemistry* sent me the message—that was the one. So I dropped it in the back of my cart and headed toward the check-out counter.

But there at the end of the aisle was an entire carousel covered with the colorful, shiny bookmarkers. They were only strips of cardboard with cords tied through the tops, but they had been printed with pretty pictures and nice little sayings about reading books and where stories can take a person. They were so nice, and I had never had one before, only a dollar, so I grabbed the shiniest one to go with my new friend.

When I walked in the back door of the house, Mark met me with a terrible frown on his face.

"Where you been, Tish?" I knew the tone. I knew what was in store for the night.

"I went to the store for some food."

"Oh good! I'm starving! What'd ya' get?"

"Fried chicken and potato salad." Then he saw my book.

"What's that? Another book? Damn, girl! You think money grows on trees? You got more books than you got roaches here! In fact, there ain't no place to even sit in this piece of shit house for all your dumb books!" He grabbed *Combustible Chemistry* out of my hands.

"Don't you bother my books, Mark. Leave 'em alone! Here. Eat some chicken. I'll pick up the house tomorrow." I pulled some paper towels off the roll to make a pretend plate and opened the paper sack containing dinner.

"Give me that!" He snatched the marker from my hand. "'Ten Reasons To Read,'" he read from the bookmarker. "Number one," his eyes looked directly into mine, and his gorgeous smile turned into a mockery of a true book lover. "Gives me a reason to sit on my fat ass all day and not clean the house!"

"Mark, give it to me." I reached my hand out to take the pretty piece of cardboard back from him.

"No. I didn't say you could buy that, or the book either." He bent the bookmarker in half, and then bent it the other way, back and forth until it broke. Then he turned on the flame on a burner of the stove and dropped my beautiful bookmarker into it.

I screamed. He ran into the living room and picked up a stack of my beloved books and dropped them in a heap on the floor. Then he reached down and picked up the first one he touched, *The Heart of the Matter*, opened it up and ripped it right in half. I felt my heart rip in two.

"You bastard! You leave my books alone!" He tore another book in half, *The Empty Bed*, and I launched myself from the kitchen right into him. That was the start of the fight. He slapped my jaw, and he punched my eye. I think I landed a few punches, and then he grabbed an empty beer bottle in one hand and grabbed a handful of my hair with the other. The bottle crashed into my head and I felt the stars explode.

"Always got your damn nose in a book and you never do a damn thing around here! No more books! Do you hear me! No more books!"

"Mark, let me go! Get out of my house!" And that's when his fist plowed into my stomach.

The rest of the night was filled with pain and ended with him pinning me to the bed and raping me. Then he rolled over, asleep before he even stopped rolling.

I remember shaking. Every part of me ached, and I cried the same tears I cried a few nights earlier. I walked into the living room and saw the destruction of my beautiful books, smelled the ashes of my colorful bookmarker. I thought about the looks I would get from the customers in the store when they see my new bruises. I thought about the pity in Lance's eyes. I couldn't stand this life anymore. I cried for my sweet prince to show up and rescue me.

I sat on the couch while Mark snored like a well-fed animal in my bed and thought about the prince that continued to hide. What could be keeping him? Had I not suffered enough for him to show up? How many more beatings did I have to take before he heard me? Could it be that Mark kept him away? Maybe if Mark were out of the picture, my prince would then be free to pull me up on his horse and carry me away to abounding love and riches.

I sobbed loudly. Let Mark wake up! I didn't give a damn. He could wake up and start beating me again—maybe that would be the one time too many that would bring my dark, sexy love to me.

I went into the kitchen, straight to the sink and shoved my

hand down through all the moldy dishes. I knew it was in there. When it sliced through the meaty part of my hand, I smiled. Yes, that was exactly what I wanted. I pulled the knife out of the bottom of the sink and walked back into the bedroom. Mark was still on his back snoring, without any knowledge or care of what I had in mind.

I stared at his face. I remembered wondering one time if he was my prince in disguise, but now I knew he could never be a prince. I raised the knife and plunged it down into his chest over and over in my own version of rape. He moaned, and his eyes opened, but at that point, he was too weak to stop me. I kept stabbing him. He turned to his belly, and I stopped, dropping the knife. He didn't move and I suddenly felt tired. The spell was broken and now my prince could come to me.

I went to the living room and picked up my books lovingly, stacking them back in their spot under the window. I would never let anyone hurt them again. Then I showered to wash his blood and smell off of me, and the memory of my revenge went down the drain with his blood.

Now looking at the room in the afternoon daylight, I spit on the floor and turn back to the living room. The sweet prince, which is my books, calls me.

2. MONDAY: MISS BITSY

Detective Jeremy Dougan headed to the station for his first day on the job in the city. After finishing the academy and putting in his time as a patrol officer, he had returned to his hometown. He finally had the career he had worked and planned for: working on the police force in his hometown as a detective. He walked into the office with a whistle on his lips and noticed a new case waiting on his rough wooden desk. Setting down his coffee, he opened the folder.

The police report told about a missing person, Anton Easley, last seen getting into his car on July 20, on the Texas A & M University campus. He had told some friends standing nearby that he planned to return to his residence to prepare for an upcoming chemistry exam. Jeremy had seen it before —an irresponsible college student suddenly decides he's not bound to anyone and takes off without letting a soul know his plans. The last known residence of the uncaring boy sent shivers of surprise through his memory: 924 Ginger Street.

Jeremy smiled. Just reading the address caused saliva to gather in his mouth. *Miss Bitsy's address.* More than fifteen years had gone by since he'd seen her. Several years earlier, Jeremy's mother had passed on the news that Miss Bitsy's husband, Uncle Eli, as the neighborhood knew him, had passed away. About a year later the news came to Jeremy that she had taken on a boarder to help with her income.

He shoved the folder into his briefcase and headed for his car to visit with his very dear old friend, and maybe score some of her famous cookies, scones, cakes, or whatever heavenly concoction had recently come out of her enchanted oven. The thought of her amazing caramel brownies suddenly sprang to mind, and he had to fight to keep from running to the parking lot. Since leaving Ginger Street, he'd never had anything like those caramel brownies.

SOON HE WAS on the sidewalk in front of her house, grinning. Little had changed in the years since he'd lived on Ginger Street. A couple of kids were wheeling around on bicycles, and across the road a little girl in yellow shorts and a flower print shirt was riding her tricycle up the driveway, shiny little streamers fluttering from the handlebars. She stopped and picked up a cat walking toward the street and plopped it on the front of the trike. *Nope, no changes here.*

Jeremy had grown up two houses down, and Miss Bitsy was the center of his world back then. The self-proclaimed grandmother of the entire community, she had cooked and baked, feeding everyone for blocks around, including the stray cats and dogs that passed her door. As he neared the house he thought the animals lounging around the yard could be the very same cats and dogs exactly where they had always been: cats in the tree grooming themselves and each other while dogs chewed bones and napped in the sun.

Staring at the front of the house, he remembered being a red-headed, freckled-faced ten-year-old boy knocking on her door. He had begged Miss Bitsy to let him do little chores because his mom didn't want him taking advantage of her. But he would never be able to remember all the times he'd sat at her Formica table in that cheery pink and yellow kitchen, eating caramel brownies and drinking a glass of milk while telling her about his day.

Whistling, he climbed the porch steps and knocked on the door. Was she still able to get around the house? She had been old back then—was she ancient now? As he stood on the porch, he almost felt the Super Mario baseball cap he used to wear. He knocked again and waited, listening for sounds coming from the other side of the door. His reward came as it creaked open, a little slower than it had all those years ago, but there she stood, almost totally unchanged.

Mrs. Mitzi Bevel, called Miss Bitsy because of her slight stature, looked through the screen. She wore a worn blue cotton dress and a well-used yellow apron that sported the stains of many ingredients in odd little shapes, an abstract painting of deliciousness. Her hair, tied neatly as always to the top of her head, had little white wispies escaping the pins. Her large-framed glasses sat on the end of her nose, and she held a wooden spoon in her hand.

Jeremy's stomach growled. "Mrs. Bevel, I'm Detective Jeremy Dougan. Do you remember me? I used to live in that house over there." He couldn't resist the boyish feeling of wanting her recognition. "I'm here to ask you a few questions about Anton Easley." He held up his badge so she could see it through the screen door.

"Jeremy Dougan? Oh, yes, Jerry, I remember you. You were the little red-headed scrap of a boy from down the road. Come in, come in! Well, what a nice surprise! How nice of you to come visit me. Oh, my… we have a lot of catching up to do." The screen door opened and she grabbed his arm and pulled him inside to her warm kitchen. She plopped him in a chair with a plate of cookies sending their sweet aroma out to the neighborhood kids. She placed a napkin in his hand and a glass of milk on the table.

Feelings of comfort flooded over him as he looked around the room at the clutter of appliances, utensils, and cookbooks. He felt right at home. Jeremy had spent countless hours in this chair looking at the mixers and books, wooden spoons and measuring cups. A cat clock's huge white eyes ticked eternally back and forth on one wall, and pictures of pink poodles decorated the wall around the window. Her cupcake canisters stood on the counter amid globs of batter, sparkly sugar and flour dust.

She perched on the chair across the table from him and began pushing other treats in his direction. "Now, tell me about what has happened to you since you've grown up."

"Well, I really need to ask you a few questions about Mr. Easley. I was told he rented a room from you."

"Oh, yes, he did. I needed to make ends meet after Eli passed away." She looked down at her lap in a quiet moment for her departed husband. "But I really want to hear about *you*, Dear. I remember you came over here nearly every day. Are you married? Do you have children?"

He grinned. "Miss Bitsy, I would have done anything for you to get a bit of those caramel brownies. I haven't had anything like them since I moved away. Yes, I'm married, but we don't have any children yet. Did Mr. Easley ever tell you he was planning a trip?"

Grinning, she launched from her chair and walked to the pantry. "I happen to have a few caramel brownies right here."

Jeremy thought drool would drip from his mouth as he

watched her come back to the table with a plate of the gooey goodness. "Boy, I hit the jackpot today!" He nearly bounced in his seat as he grabbed one and put it on his plate. "Um, back to Mr. Easley," he said. A glob of caramel stuck to his finger and he sucked it off, not wanting to waste even a molecule of the stuff.

"Well, I can't remember him ever saying anything about going anywhere. He just went to his classes and came back here. I don't think he even had very many dates. Oh… speaking of dates, you have to try my oatmeal date cake." She turned and walked to the refrigerator.

Jeremy looked at the many school pictures of children and their drawings stuck to the refrigerator door by magnets. He didn't recognize all of them, but in the upper right-hand corner, he saw his own young face next to Mark's, his best bud eons ago. "Miss Bitsy, please… you're going to ruin my supper."

"Nonsense. I remember how much you like my desserts. It's just wonderful to relive those old times."

"When was the last time you saw Anton?"

"Oh, I guess it's been a month or so. He's such a sweet boy. I actually think of him as a grandson. He even gave me a Mother's Day card last May. I think that's the first one I got in a long time. I never had children of my own, you know. I guess that's why I always enjoyed cooking for everyone in the neighborhood… sort of my way of having a family to tend to. We wanted children, but it just never happened. Did you know I used to babysit some of the kids around here?"

"Oh, yeah. I remember Mark stayed with you some after his parents broke up." Jeremy took a piece of oatmeal date cake.

"Well, I was much younger in those days. Anton and I

have been good for each other. I can't tell you what happened to him."

"We'll keep working on that mystery. This cake is wonderful! And the caramel brownies,… I think I died and went to Heaven. Miss Bitsy, you're amazing."

"Oh, thank you, Dear. It's just the same old recipe I've always had."

"Now you said you last saw Anton about a month ago?"

"Yes." She stopped and looked up the stairs as if she'd heard a noise. Her expression changed to a dark frown, then back to her sweet, smiling self, as if a cloud had crossed her face.

"Miss Bitsy, are you okay?"

She turned back and smiled. "Oh, yes, I'm fine. I just thought I heard something. Must be squirrels up there. Yes, I think it was about a month ago. I'm afraid we had a little disagreement. You see, some of my things disappeared. Oh, nothing big, but gadgets I was fond of. I'm afraid I accused him of taking them. I just can't imagine why he would want that stuff. He said he hadn't touched them, but he was the only other person here."

"Do you think he stole your stuff and left town?"

"Well, I don't know about that. I certainly wouldn't have dreamed of him taking anything from me. If he had just asked I would have given him anything."

"What things were missing?"

"Let's see… things missing… well, my rose colored Pyrex dish… my green apron… oh, my marble rolling pin, and my flour sifter."

Jeremy looked at her, incredulous at the list of missing items. The Miss Bitsy he remembered would never have made a big deal out of losing something as inconsequential as a Pyrex dish. Surely she had plenty of dishes to cook in. "Are you sure Mr. Easley took those things? What kind of monetary value did any of that have for a college student?"

"Well, I don't know why he would want them, but he was the only other person in the house; it couldn't have been anyone else. He said he didn't take them, but there was no one else here." Again she looked up the stairs as if she'd heard something, and once again a frown momentarily creased her brow.

"Miss Bitsy, let me go look for the squirrel, to pay you back for the cake and brownies."

"Oh, Jerry, I could always count on you to do little jobs for me, but I think this is a job for someone else. Don't you worry about it."

He swallowed a gulp of milk and nodded. "Exactly what did Anton say when you asked him about those items?"

"He said he didn't take them. He said I'm like his grandmother and he would never steal anything from me." She turned back to the stairs, frowning, and after a moment she stood up, shook her finger at the rooms above her head and began to yell. "You can't threaten me like that anymore, Eli Bevel! I know you're dead 'cause I killed you myself!"

That shocked Jeremy to the point of forgetting why he'd wanted to be a police officer to start with. *What?* He couldn't move or even breathe. A piece of brownie and syrupy caramel was turning to mush in his mouth. *This must be an alternate universe like The Twilight Zone or Night Gallery or something.* He was certain Rod Serling himself would come walking into the room with a cigarette between his fingers, laughing. He tried to hang on to his professionalism, but it vanished as quickly as the air rushing from a balloon.

Miss Bitsy slowly turned back to the detective and batted her eyes sheepishly. "Oh… well, I guess you heard that."

Jeremy was trying to close his mouth, but his shocked

brain slowed the process. The sweet goop fell out of his mouth, bounced off his shirt and splattered on the plate.

"All these darn ghosts around here." Then Miss Bitsy told a story that almost shut down Jeremy's senses and nearly stopped his heart.

"Eli always complained about the money I spent at the grocery store. Every time I bought groceries, he went berserk. He told me he would take my name off the checking account and start giving me an allowance if I didn't stop spending so much money on food just to give it away. I always wanted to have plenty of casseroles and cookies and pies and cakes and things like that for the neighbors. Well, I just couldn't let him stop me."

Jeremy grabbed a napkin and wiped the chocolaty mess from his mouth, chin and shirt.

"I read up on vitamins, minerals, and herbs—home remedy kinds of things—and then I just added an extra dose of potassium to his beer. When he died of a heart attack, no one questioned it. I had his funeral, collected his life insurance and bought new appliances for my kitchen."

Somewhere in the back of Jeremy's mind, a niggle of professionalism tried to return. "Miss Bitsy, I'm not sure—"

"But it turns out Eli was right. His insurance wasn't real huge, and it didn't last all that long. Soon my money ran low again. So I found a renter: Anton Easley. Oh, Anton was such a nice boy. I loved him, and he loved me. He fixed broken things for me, ate my cooking and did all kinds of little chores around here. I was the happiest I had ever been."

"Miss Bitsy, you're the kindest, sweetest person I know." Jeremy couldn't quite process the story coming from her in that pink and yellow room with sunshine beaming in through the window like warm water.

"One day I heard that Mrs. Biggers around the corner, that

her son—you remember Clint? —And daughter-in-law had a baby, and I wanted to take her something to celebrate. Only, my Pyrex wasn't in the cabinet. I couldn't find it anywhere.

"I asked Anton about the dish, and he denied that he had touched it. He said he didn't even know where I kept it. But the thing is, like I said before, he and I were the only ones in the house and the dish was not in the cabinet or the dish-washer. I knew he must have put it somewhere. If he hadn't lied about it, I would have believed he'd just put it up in the wrong place.

"And then my apron was gone. I wondered whether he was playing jokes on me by hiding my dish and my apron. When I want to cook a casserole, the first things I do are get out my rose-colored Pyrex and put on my green apron—green for nutritional food. I wear the yellow apron for cooking sweets since yellow is so cheery. My pink apron is for bread since bread is comforting, like pink. I wear the blue apron when I'm cooking for someone who needs a meal brought to them to help brighten their day because they feel… well, blue."

Jeremy pushed his plate away. His appetite had left him with grief in his stomach. A thought rolled through his mind.

She's gotten away with Eli's murder for years, so why arrest her now? It would mean digging him up and doing all the forensics to find the proof. Surely there could be no harm in forgetting what he had heard.

"Anyway, I wanted to make a casserole, but I couldn't find my Pyrex or my green apron. Anton swore he didn't know anything about them, but I knew he was lying." Her face began to change again as she took on a determined look. "I thought if I could sweeten him up, he might tell me what he did with them, so I decided to make a cobbler. I put on my happy yellow apron and pulled out my cobbler dish, mixed up the piecrust, and realized my beautiful, heavy marble rolling pin had also disappeared.

"I asked Anton about that, and he told the same lie, said he didn't know what had happened to it. He said he saw me put it in the refrigerator to make it cold so my crust wouldn't stick to it, but when I looked in the refrigerator it wasn't there. I told Anton I knew he had taken it and I wanted it back. I told him these little jokes he was playing on me weren't funny. He said he honestly didn't know where the items had gone. I figured he took them to a friend's house or something. And then when the flour sifter vanished, well, I got angry. It was just a little sifter, but out of the three I own, that one worked the best. The other two have little bits of flour permanently stuck in them."

Miss Bitsy's face began to look sad and dark. She shook her head. "Too think, I loved him so much, and he could steal from me and then lie about it. I was utterly heartbroken. I cried for two days over the fact that he would do that to me. Well, I knew I couldn't let him get away with it. Those were just piddly little things, but he had no right to hide them somewhere."

The cop came back to life in Jeremy's head as he sat at the table sucking up tears. "Miss Bitsy, do you realize what you're saying?"

"I'd gone to the basement on a hunting expedition for my things when I remembered that the second step from the top bowed in the middle. Eli used to tell me to be careful and not step on it. 'Walk lightly, for heaven's sake, Woman,' he would say. You know, I don't know why he never fixed it. Oh well, water under the bridge. The day I was hunting for my stuff, I stepped on it again. It sank a little deeper than I remembered and made a creaking noise. I knew at that moment what I had to do to keep Anton from stealing any more of my things."

Jeremy tried to think of the thousands of moments he'd spent in this chair in this kitchen telling his dear friend about his day at school and how the teacher had marked up his paper just to be mean. He had gone to Miss Bitsy's after the Carson boys beat him up and stole his baseball cards. He had run to her house the night his parents had the fight that ended their marriage. And she always had a hug, a glass of milk and a caramel brownie for him. But now that she wanted to tell him about a terrible day in her life, all he could think of was that he should be arresting her.

"I went back up the stairs and put my frozen meatloaf in the oven for supper, and then I went back down the stairs. I got Eli's old saw from his workbench and went to work on that bad step. Just about an inch of sawing in the middle and my trick was set."

Jeremy tried to say something else. He felt as if a whip were lashing at his back. He opened his mouth to beg her to stop talking, stop leading him down this road to hell, but he also had a sudden fascination, as if a train were exploding in front of him.

"Anton came in from his class just as the food came out of the oven and we sat down to a nice meal of meatloaf, mashed potatoes and gravy, and sugared green beans with applesauce cake for dessert. After we ate, he kissed me on the cheek and handed me his rent money. I folded it up and put it in the pocket of my orange apron, the one I wear when all the others are in the wash."

"Miss Bitsy!" Jeremy finally croaked. "Please...I'm a *policeman*... a *detective*. Please don't tell me any more. I'll have to take you downtown."

She didn't seem to hear a word. In fact, she looked up into empty space as if Anton had just kissed her cheek. She reached one hand out and took a piece of air, which the detective assumed was Anton's rent money. "I asked him, 'Anton, would you be a sweetie and run down in the basement to see if you can find Eli's old hammer so I can crush up some hard candies? Old Man Arthur has been creeping around in my spine lately, and I'm afraid to try the stairs right now.'" She was speaking to the space between her and the squirming detective. "Oh, he scampered off like a schoolboy." She actually smiled as if watching him scamper all over again. "He opened the basement door and clicked on the light, and I heard his heavy foot plop down on the first little step. The second step gave way with a loud crack, and he yelled as he fell to the concrete floor" She looked at the basement door and called, "'Oh, Anton, I forgot to warn you about that step. Stay still, Dear. I'll be right there.'"

While Miss Bitsy was looking away, Jeremy took the moment to wipe his eyes, using considerable effort to keep from sobbing out loud.

"Well, I went to the pantry and picked up Eli's hammer where I had hidden it earlier and went to the top of the stairs. 'Are you still there?'" She cocked her head with her hand behind her ear as if listening for something, acting out her deeds. "'Anton, are you okay?' There was no sound, so I went down to the shape on the floor." She looked at the kitchen floor. "He wasn't conscious, but I didn't see any blood, so he wasn't hurt too badly. I patted his cheek." She patted the air near the floor.

Jeremy shuddered.

"'Anton?' He opened one bloodshot eye, and a little pink tinge of spit came out of his mouth. "Where's my Pyrex, my apron, my rolling pin, and my sifter?' His eyes opened wide, and he shifted back and forth. 'I know you did something with them, and I want them back.' He still didn't say anything, but he raised his hands as if a fly were buzzing around him. 'Last time, Anton. Where are they?' He tried to push himself away with his legs, but one was bent kind of strange. I raised the hammer and… well…" She raised her fist in the air and her lips curled, contorting her sweet face to resemble that of a monster. Her hand, closed around the imaginary hammer, swooshed down in an arc, bludgeoning Anton again and again. "*I put! Poor! Anton! Out! Of his misery!*"

A sob blurted from Jeremy's soul. He cried miserably, "Miss Bitsy! No! No, no, no, no!" He raised his head, gaining a slight bit of control. "Is Anton in your basement, Miss Bitsy?"

"No. He's not there anymore." Her face had changed again. She looked tired and sad. She looked down at her lap, then over to the chest freezer.

"Is he in your freezer?" Jeremy shook his head from side to side, denying a horrible truth but wondering how much more horror this day had in store.

"More or less."

He walked to the freezer, lifted the lid and looked in. About a hundred white packages lay in piles neatly inside the arctic chamber. He looked at Miss Bitsy, searching for the courage to ask the question had to ask.

"I knew he would stink down there, but he was too big for me to drag him back up, especially after the step was broken. So I took my electric carving knife and cut him into pieces that I could wrap up and carry to the freezer. Then I scrubbed the floor down there with bleach to clean up the… well, you know."

"You said, 'more or less.' Dear God, please tell me you're not eating him." The sweets he had eaten wanted freedom and he gagged at the thought of her committing cannibalism.

"Oh, heavens no!" She chuckled. "Every day I take out a package and thaw it. Then I take a bit of Anton, slice him up and let the dogs and cats from the neighborhood have him. He always loved all those animals. I know he would have like that."

Reaching into his pocket, he pulled out the small two-way radio and rubbed the button. Miss Bitsy, the champion of his childhood, his confidante and friend—how could he turn her in? He lowered the radio, and then brought it back up. He had taken an oath to uphold the laws of the community. She might kill again. Once again he lowered the radio. She was an old woman and probably didn't realize what she had done. But her final question to Anton continued to buzz in his brain, freezing everything he had ever believed about her: *Last time, Anton. Where are they?* He raised the radio and pushed the button.

"Go ahead," the dispatcher said.

He sucked in a breath of air along with the teary snot threatening to run to his mouth. "Please send a squad car to 924 Ginger Street." He looked back at Miss Bitsy, who appeared to shimmer through his hot tears.

She was at the kitchen counter, bustling around the kitchen, preparing to create another culinary masterpiece. She reached into the cabinet by her head and pulled out a rose-colored Pyrex dish and a green apron. Then she turned around and one hand went to her mouth. "Oh, Jerry! I'm so glad you've come to see me! What will it be today? Oatmeal cake or caramel brownies?"

3. TUESDAY: THE OLD HOUSE

The old house sits back off the road on its own little acre of land, a field of overgrown weeds, thistles, and scrub. It sits there doing nothing, but it taunts me. The gray hulk looks as ancient as I feel, a monument to the history it holds. From where I stand on the road, the weathered gray looks almost black in the sunlight. The house stands alone on this road, but there were neighbors—once.

As I look at the house and dread what must take place. My mind goes back in time. The sunburned gray wood of the siding becomes gleaming white showing the sparkling promise of the future. The shutters and screen door are painted a rich blue, the color of peace. I see Benjamin Vaughn, the young owner of the house, standing on the road, watching as the builders put the finishing touches of white on the wood. His thoughts are strong in the air, imagining the beautiful woman he will soon possess. He shouts to the workers in a harsh voice that his bride, the beautiful Corrine, must be absolutely thrilled with his house. His house must match her beauty board for board, no imperfections whatsoever. I shudder as I listen to his egotistical tirade.

In the midst of the ancient activity to finish the construction, the yard also transforms itself into a carpet of green; its beds of ivy and roses encircling the house. In the middle of the yard, the withered oak tree greens and straightens, crying out for lovers to picnic beneath it and children to play in its branches. The smell of the grass and flowers return to me and erase the dryness of decay. Young Benjamin breathes in the perfumes and is satisfied with his new home.

I am propelled forward a few weeks and I watch Benjamin carrying his bride up the pathway. The second-floor window is open and blue curtains flap as if welcoming, waving to them. The white lace of Corrine's gown is in sharp contrast to the deep black of Benjamin's suit. Her face shines with bliss, but his is set in determination and triumph, as if he has won a prize. As I watch them disappear into the house, reality returns. Oh, God, have I not been through this enough! I have watched this over and over through the years and always beg for my grave at the end of the day.

I walk up the path through the yard, grass and scrub crunching beneath my feet. I struggle in the heat of the day as the sun beats down on me in relentless punishment. I falter in the heat, but no relief comes. I know I must make this walk.

Reaching the porch, I notice the posts have begun to lean out toward the yard. It won't be long before they give way altogether and allow the roof to meet the ground. Rocking chairs on either side of the door still wait for their owners to sit in the evening breeze and watch their children play in the yard and climb the oak tree. The chairs were once privy to plans for the future as Benjamin sat with Corrine and enjoyed his yard, breathing the scents of roses and grass while watching the misty rain of a summer afternoon.

Benjamin is sitting there now, close to the door, enjoying a fine cigar, still dressed in his wedding suit while Corrine is inside preparing herself for his embrace. His face shines with pride in anticipation of claiming her as his possession. He rocks in the chair with his head held high.

My hand reaches for the screen and feels the splintering of the rotting wood. How I hate to enter, but I must carry on. The door opens into the front room where the sun shines hatefully through the dirt-streaked window and moth-eaten draperies, magnifying dust particles in the air. The stained wallpaper peels in spots while the furniture rots away, gaping with holes where rodents have burrowed for shelter from the weather. The ancient grandfather clock still stands against the east wall; its pendulum stilled for eternity. A small skeleton, perhaps a mouse, lies scattered across the floor. I hear in my head the ghostly echoes of the old nursery rhyme, "Hickory, Dickory, Dock," a mockery of the past as if children had actually lived here to sing and play. Cobwebs drape the corners of the ceiling, a macabre veil covering the odors of dry animal dung and dust that fills my nose.

My heart sinks as I view the waste and remember the beauty and comfort of this room. I can see the wallpaper, white with stripes of tiny flower bouquets, gleaming in the sunlight. The holes in the couch heal themselves and the dust and dirt dissolve to reveal lush, blue upholstery. The cobwebs vanish and the floorboards shine with the luster of care. The clock pendulum rocks back and forth, and I hear the seconds ticking by.

How I wish I could stop that ticking and suspend this moment in time. This room should be remembered this way. The curtains over the window are tied back and the glass is raised so that I hear the creaks as young Benjamin rocks on the porch. I close my eyes and smell cigar smoke mixed with roses. His arrogance and pride grieve me. I hear his bride's voice from upstairs calling that she is ready for him. Through the open window I see him smile, rise, extinguish his cigar, and go to meet her.

The scene fades. Once again I am back in the rotting room, the stifling heat crushing me. Now I must climb the stairs, so I place my hand on the newel post. Above the staircase, a piece of the roof has given way allowing the weather in to eat at the risers, and it will ultimately claim the entire house. I am relieved at that thought. When this house is gone, I will be free. But for now, I must go up.

I test each riser to see if my weight will be supported, listening for creaks that become screams. The velvety wood of the banister is covered with dirt, so I can't lean on that for support either. I must stay to the center, careful of the bits of fallen roof.

As I reach the second-floor landing, I look at the four doors flanking the hall. One leads to a toilet room, one to a guest bedroom, one to an empty nursery, and one to the master bedroom. This last room is where I am headed. I put my hand on the crystal doorknob and twist. The door opens easily for me, as I knew it would.

The room before me is bright with sunlight and oppressive with heat. This room sits directly above the front room, and across from me is the window with the once waving curtains, now turned to rags. A bed with a wrought iron frame stands against the wall under the window; its mattress is stained and full of holes, aged brown stuffing poking through and filled with mouse droppings. The wardrobe stands across from the bed, blackened with age, its wood melting together. Next to the door stands a dressing table topped by a mirror; the silver backing has browned and begun to run, drawing macabre stripes in the glass. The flocked paper on the walls is peeling and an odor of musk hangs in the air.

This was the room where the lovers slept. He claimed her

and kept her here—she became his and he would never let her go—and he took pleasure from her physical delights. She slept with her head on his chest, trusting the safety in the strength of his arms; and his head moved to breathe the perfume of her hair. They lived in this world and that world was complete and closed. As he slept, he dreamed of the children they would one day have to complete the appearance.

I leave the phantom lovers locked in their embrace and softly close the door behind me. My next stop waits directly across the hall: the nursery. Dear God, no! This is the room where the madness begins. The usual pain starts in my chest as my palm sweats. I reach for the doorknob. The door swings open and I stare across the empty room through the window overlooking the backyard. An unused crib rests against the east wall, and like the rest of the house, time and neglect have claimed it. The weight of dust has caused the bottom to fall to the floor.

My eyes sting with tears as I cross to the window to gaze at the yard. Now, more jungle than a yard, I peer through the overgrowth and locate the line where the laundry hung to dry, soaking up sunshine and fresh air. I blink away my tears and watch Corrine, her belly rounded with the future, hanging her sheets. A man steps through the fence hedge. He speaks to her and she answers him and smiles.

The air in the room changes and I realize Benjamin now stands behind me watching the scene in the yard. I can feel his madness electrifying the air as everything around me grows faint. I want to scream at him of the terrible waste that is looming, that his anger and jealousy are unjustified. But of course, I can't. He is a vision of the past and cannot hear me. I hear him whisper that she must be punished. She must learn that she belongs to him and no one else, and the man in the yard must never return.

I leave him standing there and turn to walk from the room. I have one more room to visit before my task is complete for another year. I turn with fear and mourning, ordering my heavy feet to move. The stairs are waiting for me.

On the bottom floor directly across from the landing, there is a hallway leading to the kitchen and dining area. After all these years, I should expect the scene of decay, but my breath catches at the waste. Something small skitters across the floor and I recoil. I know nothing can hurt me here, but my sense of disgust is still strong.

There are windows on the west wall—they are part of this story—and they admit the merciless sunlight. Standing in the doorway, I can no longer hold back my grief and a sob escapes. This is the room where the horror played out and tears stream down my face as I gather the courage to face what is to come. Here the horror will play out once again.

The curtains that once covered the grimy windows now lay on the floor; time has released them from their fixture. A small pine table surrounded by four chairs stands against the wall next to the doorway. A cook stove takes up the corner against the east wall. Once gleaming with white enamel, it is now covered with dirt and rust spots. The west wall holds the three windows, cabinets and a sink. Above the sink, a window has been smashed scattering broken glass across the bottom of the sink and onto the wooden floor. Twigs, leaves, dirt, and rocks litter all the surfaces. A few steps from the sink a shapeless stain mars the floor, and a dirty, wadded piece of crochet rests against the wall.

I step into the room; one step is almost more than I can bear. This, Young Benjamin's favorite room, welcoming him home from work each day with its warm stove and delicious smells, is now the most dreadful room in the house. In his narrow little world where everything was so perfect, imperfection and horror were about to creep in and destroy him.

Looking out the window and I see Benjamin coming in from a day of work at the bank in town. He is whistling and the sun is shining. Corrine, beautiful in spite of the fading bruise on her face in the shape of his hand, sits at the table, enjoying a cup of coffee in the sunshine, but she is not alone. The neighbor, Mr. Hadley, sits across from her, feasting on one of her pastries. The gleaming windows are open, and Benjamin hears the tinkle of her laughter as he walks up the path. His face darkens and I feel the jealousy emanating out from him like ocean waves.

Clouds cover the sun with freakish speed and the flowers bordering the walk seem to droop in sadness. He quickens his step to reach the house and disappears as he enters the front door. A moment later he enters the kitchen and the air freezes. Suddenly my head and chest feel as if they will burst.

Corrine looks up and introduces Mr. Hadley, stating that he came to bring a gift he thought she would find useful in her condition, and she points to the little-crocheted rug on the floor in front of the sink. Mr. Hadley stands to shake hands with Benjamin, noting the darkness on his face. The tension is so thick a knife would stick fast in the air.

Benjamin glares at the intruder and demands to know his intentions. Mr. Hadley's face pales and becomes blank with confusion. He begs the young man's pardon and leaves the room, Benjamin, and Corrine facing each other. She drops her eyes from his, knowing what he is capable of. A barrage of verbal abuse and accusations pour from his lips as she tries to calm him. Trying to divert his attention, she turns to the sink and hands her husband a bowl of potatoes to wash and peel for dinner, then heads to the stove to tend to a different task.

I can see the madness in his face, and the jealousy turns

his skin shades of green. The memory of her sitting at the table with another man, laughing and sipping coffee, causes his eyes to blur. She belongs to him and he doesn't like to share his possessions. He turns to hurl another insult at her, accentuating the syllable of his own dark reason by stabbing the air with the knife he holds. She answers quietly with her eyes averted and hesitantly crosses the room to take the potatoes from him.

"Stop! Don't move from the stove!" I scream aloud at her from my point across the room. But I know what happens next, just as I know the sun stopped shining on that horrible day.

As she reaches for the bowl his arm darts out and grabs her, the bowl crashes to the floor. He twists her arm around.

She screams out. "Benjamin, you're hurting me! The Baby, Benjamin, the baby!" The terror in her voice freezes the blood in my veins. Why can't her husband hear that fear and pleading?

"It is mine, isn't it?" He taunts her. "You are mine and I WILL NOT have another man in my house!" His other hand comes around to slap her, but he has forgotten the knife he holds with that hand. The blade grazes her cheek and she screams. I feel my bones melting and wonder how many more times I must watch this scene.

"Oh, God, Benjamin, stop! Let me go! Help!"

I discover that I, myself, am screaming. "Let her go! Don't do it! Let her go!" I run across the room to tackle him, forgetting that they are images long past. Benjamin's hand with the knife pulls away from her face and plunges into her chest.

Instantly I feel the crushing pain. My heart is bursting and I can't breathe. Corrine sinks to the floor and gasps for air. "Benj…" she breathes. Her eyelids flutter and then close.

I am sick. My stomach threatens to empty out.

Benjamin looks at the still body of his wife and unborn child and awareness dawns on his face. "No. No. NO. NO," is all he can repeat and the rafters tremble. Not only is Corrine gone, but so is the child, his namesake, who would carry the name into the future. The whole world has ended. He turns his head to the window as if he hears a noise and sees Mr. Hadley. The crime has been witnessed from start to finish.

I am utterly exhausted. Reliving this always leaves me spent and unable to move for a time. I lay on the floor sobbing, crying for my lost Corrine. I did love her very much. She was beautiful—perfect—and I was a horrible monster.

My trial was quick, and the sentence carried out in haste. I was hanged by the neck until dead, but that was not the end. Because of my jealousy, my love of perfection, my insanity, I must walk through this house and relive the day each year on the anniversary of her death.

So, for one more year, my misery is complete.

4. WEDNESDAY: THE EPIC BATTLE

Finally, he heaved a sigh of relief. It was over. The whole thing was behind him. Now he would be ready for tomorrow.

It was hard to believe that five minutes earlier Brett had been sure his death had come to meet him. Five minutes ago he faced the monster head on and stood his ground, tapping the heroic attitude that this satanic demon would never take his soul. He faced the angel from hell and the fight began.

Five minutes before this epic battle he sat on the bathroom floor backed into a corner and cringing like a young child. No! No! It couldn't be real! He pinched himself in an effort to wake up, but only created a bruise. The horror still stared at him.

Five minutes before he realized this monster actually existed, he had been in the kitchen eating a fine meal with his wife and kids: pork chops with applesauce, garlic mashed potatoes, broiled asparagus, and he knew carrot cake was for dessert. His favorite meal; Cassie must have a special night planned. She had carefully cultivated his anticipation. He would enjoy his meal then give her his undivided attention.

And then, between a bite of potatoes and a drink from his glass, one of the kids asked to be excused to the restroom. "Sure, go ahead," he had answered with a smile.

Five minutes before that wondrous meal which would lead to the wonderful evening coming up, Brett pulled into the driveway after a day at the office. His job was going well and he didn't have a care in the world. The promotion looked right in line right where it should have been; his work for the month was finished; all the customers loved him and asked for him personally instead of taking the next person in line. What in the world could knock him down now! He smiled and left his car.

Now, these twenty minutes later, he had learned what endurance and strength really meant. He looked at his handiwork, the remnants of the beast left laying on the floor, Cassie and the kids standing in the hallway with eyes as round as the plates on the dinner table. He grabbed a piece of toilet paper to soak the sweat from his forehead. They knew. They knew his weakness. Correction, they knew his PAST weakness. Never again would he feel faint when facing a monster of this type.

Thinking back to the battle that had ended in the bathroom two minutes earlier, his trembling began. Tina, the child that had been excused from the table, had screamed and Brett, the father and defender of the home, ran to her side. He saw the intruder and suddenly felt faint himself. Of all evil things in the world, why did he have to face this one? But his daughter's screaming little voice cut through the fear. "Kill it, Daddy! Kill it!"

He had stared at the vile creature as Cassie put the weapon in his hand. This was the moment of truth. Could he, Brett Foster, master of the banking world, protector of the House of Foster, face his biggest fear and kill the terror that threatened to take his home, his family, his daughter? He raised his weapon and took a step closer. IT rose up as if to look him in the face. He could almost hear the hiss of its voice.

"Come get me, scaredy boy!"

He had backed against the wall, his weaponed hand lowering without his consent. "I can't do it! I can't! No way! It'll just go away if I leave it alone."

"Daddy, I believe in you." Tina leaned over and brushed her lips against her daddy's ear.

A light exploded in his brain so that he almost lost his vision again. He WAS the master. He was the builder of the house, the provider and protector of the home, and his darling little Tina had faith in her daddy. How dare this demon threaten his daughter! He would hang its giblets from the porch to show any others that came along that he was the boss of his turf!

He raised his weapon one more time and a look of supreme determination gelled on his face.

"NO SPIDERS ALLOWED IN MY HOUSE!!" And he had slapped the arachnid with the force of a dynamite explosion sending it to oblivion.

He heaved another sigh of relief as five hundred nearly invisible black spots left their dead mother and looked for dark corners in which to hide.

5. THURSDAY: LAURA'S RETURN

I saw her again today. I always knew she'd come back and that's why I stayed here. Just one sight of her was enough to make me glad I waited. One heavenly glimpse of her beauty and sparkle and I knew the world would be right again. And I intend to make it better.

She looked a little different—not older—in fact, she looked as young as ever. Her golden hair fell to the middle of her back glistening as if the sun's rays came from her instead of the sky. How I've missed touching her hair, running my fingers through the gloss and feeling it slip through my hand… well, just before. And it wasn't tied up on top of her head, but flowing like a golden waterfall.

She wore some shocking garments. She left this house in her dark blue dressing gown. I remember distinctly because the dressing gown was the same color as her eyes, and when they closed, I wanted to pull the color from the robe and put it back where it belonged. What a horrible night that was! I didn't want to think of it again, but I have been unable to think of anything else since.

She walked into the house carrying a large box and

wearing very little: blue britches short enough to show her legs from her heavenly thighs all the way to her feet. I had to look away because I couldn't trust myself not to do something imbecilic. And the blouse she wore looked like a man's undershirt with some sort of writing across her breasts. A little embarrassed for her, I wanted to find the blue dressing gown to cover her. But who knows what she went through since leaving here.

The box she carried was large and she walked into the room across from what was once our bedroom. She planted the box on the bed and I watched as she removed the contents: books and toys, mostly, a few other clothes, and some small trinkets. How she loved her trinkets. Our mantel had been covered with glass ornaments and pictures of this and that, lacy fans and feathers, and the dagger… yes, well… she loved her little baubles. And I tried to furnish her all the little pretties this house could hold.

She walked around the room, her shimmering hair bouncing around her shoulders, humming a tune I didn't recognize. I wondered if she still played the piano and harpsichord. Was music still as important to her as it once was? She had the sweetest soprano voice, able to bring tears to angels' eyes. My darling Laura was the toast of the country with her musical talents.

That was the medium through which I met her the first time. She performed at the opera house, solo, and I attended with friends in an effort to escape the pain of a broken youth's heart. I never expected to replace the previous trollop with an angel straight from heaven. And when she consented to be my bride, I almost knew I heard angels singing. I don't know what happened for our lives to turn so wrong. I've hoped and prayed for years upon years that she would forgive me and return.

And there she was, dancing around the bedroom in her undergarments, almost as if she were begging me to take her. I had to leave the doorway and stand with my face pressed into the wall to cool the passion that threatened to take over. I loved her with every ounce of my being and we had shared some very intimate times. We were man and wife and committed no sin, and I hoped for children. Little did I know what was to come.

She came through the doorway and I flattened into the wall trying not to be noticed—not yet. My time would come. But she passed me and kept dancing down the hall toward the stairs. I could only stand there and absorb the feel of her essence.

I'd longed to see her again forever! As soon as she left all those years ago, a panic set deep in my heart and I feared I might go mad with grief and pain. But as the years passed and the traces of her faded, the grief ebbed to some degree. I would never walk to the end of the front stairs again, never be able to pass the spot on the floor where her last breath was exhaled. But after a time I was able to use the back stairs. In that way, I navigated through the house quite easily.

But through it all, I never doubted that she would be back. Her passing from that long ago world was just a stage and she would find a way to return. I've stayed here waiting through every tick of the clock downstairs, and even after the hands stopped moving across the face. Time didn't stop just because the pendulum stilled its sway. The leaves on the trees outside continued to bud Tand grow, green with vibrancy, wither and fall.

Just as I pondered the time I spent waiting for her return, Laura came back up the stairs with another box. There were wires attached to her head through her ears and she sang strange words to another unknown tune. I could see the words painted across her breasts: A Day to Remember. Was she mocking me? Did she return with the intention of constantly reminding me of that night and the pain that followed? Is that why she took her belongings to the room across from ours?

A man's voice called up the stairs. "Laura! Laura! Turn off the IPod! Come get your rug!"

A man. There was a man moving in with her. Pain flashed through my head and the same old visions filled my eyes once again. The opera house. The carriage and horses. A drink in the pub. Water splashing on my shoes. I arrive home and there's a light in our bedroom window.

She hadn't felt well and I went to the program with my colleague, Peter. After the show, Peter and I went for a drink. From the pub, I said goodbye to him and headed home to a bride of less than a year. I walked in the door and heard noises coming from my room upstairs: laughter from male and female. A blackness covered my eyes as I grabbed her dagger from the mantel and raced up the stairs. Her scream, his moan as I plunged the blade into his bare back.

I stared at him bleeding on my sheets, Laura in her blue robe. I turned for the stairs, intent on leaving the house to compose myself before coming back, but she followed at my heels screaming and sobbing.

"Frederick! Frederick! Stop! Listen to me!" Standing on the top landing, I was confused about my next move. She put her hands out to me, those hands that had been wrapped around her lover only a moment earlier.

"You whore!" I screamed at her while pushing her back, pushing her back to the balcony, pushing her over the balustrade to the floor.

A quick sound left her mouth, then the thud—Oh, God, that sickening crunch—as she hit the floor. I stood there with grief pouring from my eyes and heart while I listened to her struggle to draw a breath. The passion was leaving my mind and devastation took its place. She lay broken to bits on the floor below me and a red circle grew under her head.

I ran down the stairs and stooped to her. "Oh, Laura. I'm so sorry. Forgive me. Forgive me. Laura, for—"

Then it happened. She drew one soggy breath as the red bubbles leaked from the side of her mouth. "Fre—" and that beautiful blue light left her eyes. I knew she was gone.

Then I heard a voice from somewhere inside my skull. "She'll be back. You'll see. She'll be back." Was that when the madness began? Was that the moment? Can one look back to the single moment in time when sanity snaps and the world shatters taking reality away?

I laughed. It started with a quiet giggle that bubbled up my throat. But that quiet little giggle soon joined with other giggles and chuckles and then full-out laughter. I laughed for hours with the new knowledge that she would return. I knew this as solidly as I knew my name. I ran up the stairs to look at my other handiwork.

The gentleman that had become intimate with my wife had moved himself around a little and he was making noises, pain-filled moans. Laughing like the loon I had become, I took the dagger and stabbed him over and over—I have no idea how many times. Soon he did not move or make any sounds. Soon even the blood stopped.

Leaving the room, I headed down the back stairs, out to the shed where I had a perfect piece of rope. I returned to the front staircase and hanged myself from the very balustrade I had pushed my angel from. My laughter ceased, the ticking of the clock stopped. When the bright light came for me, I refused to follow. I knew my Laura would be back and I determined to wait for her.

And today she returned. With another man. I glided

through the wall into her room as she was emptying the new box she had brought up.

"Laura," I whispered. A strand of her hair waved at me in response to my breath. "Laura, I have waited for you and you have returned to me."

She didn't acknowledge me; the unpacking and singing continued. "Laura. Laura, look at me." Gliding to the space in front of her and mustering all the strength I could, I made myself visible. I know she saw me. I know it because of the horror that was borne on her face and spread to her blue eyes. "Laura, don't scream. I've waited for you." Her eyes grew ever larger and her mouth, that sweet cave of nectar, opened wide. "Sshh. Laura, it is I, your husband. I've waited for you for over a century. Now you're here." The pain returned to me with the single scream that jumped from her throat.

"Daddy! Daddy! This house is haunted! There's a ghost in my room! Oh, Daddy!" And she ran for the stairs screaming.

Fading back into the wall, my heart broke all over again. Afraid of me. My darling was afraid of me. I can never have her like that. My dear angelic Laura. I only wanted to be your husband. I only wanted a married life and children, then old age and death sweetly together. But I cannot force myself upon you. I cannot force you to love me as I love you. I must now try to leave this house and search out an end to my torture.

6. FRIDAY: MAGGIE'S WEDDING

I fluffed the ribbons of my bouquet; it had to be perfect for Maggie's wedding. She had chosen the colors "eggplant purple" and "champagne gold," beautiful, elegant colors that I would have chosen myself if it had been me.

And it should have been me. Eric was mine. We started seeing each other during the last year he was married; we were together during his divorce, and we were still together. In fact, he had just left my bed the night before Maggie called me to announce their engagement.

"Val, can you come help me with this garter thing?" Very carefully, I put the bouquet on a shelf, making sure the ribbons stayed fluffed out and turned to my best friend, who was sitting on the chair behind me holding the elasticized lace. The skirt of her gown was layers and layers of tule that she would never be able to get through on her own.

I loved Maggie. Best friends since high school, she never seemed to realize that we came from two different worlds. My parents were simple business people—a banker and a secretary—working and saving, always just barely enough money to make ends meet. Maggie's parents—a lawyer and a real estate agent with wealthy backgrounds—seemed to make plenty of money to mix with what they inherited. As friends, money was never an issue between us and we were like sisters.

I looked at her standing in front of the mirror. Her long red hair was swept up from her neck to the top of her head.

She didn't know how much I loved Eric because she never knew about our love affair. I was the one there for him when his wife found out about me and kicked him out. I was there while she fought him so hard in the courtroom. I was the one there for him when his kids went back to his ex-wife after weekend visits with him. And I was there when he needed a woman's touch.

When Eric and I started seeing each other, I could never mention him to Maggie, even after she told me she met him. Maggie's mother had divorced her father because of adultery on his part, and Maggie still hated the other woman, now her step-mother. She had said so many horrible things about her father and step-mother that I could never tell her because I was no different from her step-mother.

After Eric's divorce I couldn't bring it up; by the time it was all over and the dust cleared, he was my secret, and there was romance and danger in keeping a secret like Eric from Maggie. She could have anything she ever wanted. I kept thinking Eric was the one thing I had that she didn't. There were so many times I tried to tell her about the new love of my life, but my tongue seemed glued to the roof of my mouth; so I kept Eric to myself.

We usually only met on the weekends, taking turns between my apartment and his. Those were sweet meetings. Eric was so romantic, sexy and mysterious, exactly the adventure I wanted. And when I fell for him, he told me he felt the same. He said his whole life revolved around me. I knew breaking up his marriage was wrong, but I also knew I needed him. No matter what it took, we needed to be together.

One weekend he was at my apartment and teased me about keeping him a secret from my friends.

"Like this girl," he said holding Maggie's picture. I looked at the picture of her; red hair swirled around her green turtle-necked sweatered shoulders, green eyes reflecting her laughing smile. I remembered the day that picture was taken. We were Christmas shopping and she had tried on a pair of outrageous shoes, parading around the store like a starving model.

"She wouldn't understand what we have."

"Why not?"

"She would hate me forever because I was the reason your marriage broke up."

"Val, I told you, my marriage had been over for a while. You simply helped Brenda see that. Now tell me about this picture."

I told him we were friends from high school, that she came from a fairly well-off family, and that she was like a sister to me. He put the picture back in its place on top of the television.

I STOOD LOOKING at myself in the dark purple maid-of-honor gown holding the ever-so-slightly golden tinged flowers of my bouquet while standing in front of the dressing room mirror in the church. The flowers had to be just right today.

Rehearsal had been the night before and I knew my role: last of the attendants to enter the sanctuary before the flower girl and ring bearer, right before Maggie and her step-father. I was to be there for her and make sure her dress displayed her glory as the bride, hold her bouquet when the time came to exchange the rings, and assist her in leaving the stage to light the unity candle. And when she and Eric, her husband, turned to leave the auditorium, I would once again help her with her dress. After the children left the room, I would be the first attendant to take the arm of the best man and leave. I would assist her all during the reception, and like every other single girl, try my best to catch the bride's bouquet, hoping for a groom of my own.

Once again I surveyed my appearance. No hair was out of place. A professional had applied my makeup and it was perfect without looking overdone. The dress was flawless. I practiced facial expressions, trying to affect "the happy best friend" look. An inspection of the bouquet showed no glint of irregularity. Everything looked perfect. And Maggie was next in line for the mirror, so I moved away.

Not long after Eric had asked me about Maggie, she told me about meeting him, talked on and on about what a perfect gentleman he was, never realizing that I was nearly sick. He was sexy, mysterious and romantic. With a smile on my face, I told her how wonderful and magical their story was.

Maggie had been leaving a restaurant and the taxi pulled over. As she opened the door near the sidewalk, he opened the door on the street, so they shared the ride. She left the cab first and he got a glimpse of the lavish apartment building where she lives, so he asked for her phone number.

"But Maggs, you don't know anything about him! He could be a serial killer!"

"I'm a big girl and I can make my own decisions. I've thought all that through and I'm going to take a chance. When I handed him my phone number, he touched my hand so tenderly and it was so warm! I'll go out with him once, just to see what he's like—if he calls me, that is."

My mouth opened once more to tell her I knew him, been sleeping with him for three years, but all that came out was, "I just don't want you to get hurt. You know I love you like a sister."

"Well don't worry about me. I'll go out with him one time and keep my 'weird radar' on full blast."

When I confronted Eric about it, he told me he was after that money. He would get close to her and run his hands through her money, just to pay off a couple of bills. Then he would drop her. We would run away together and live happily ever after.

Horrified, I told him I couldn't stand that; I told him I wanted him all to myself. But even more than that, I didn't want her hurt; she was closer to me than my sister.

We stood on my balcony in the moonlight and he put his hands on my face and kissed me. His fingers brushed the ticklish spot behind my ears, spreading fire through me. But my tears kept running in a river.

Breaking from the embrace, I went as far from him on the balcony as I could get. "No! No. I can't do this. I don't care how much money you think you can get from her. And she *will* get hurt. Don't you see how you're killing both of us?"

"Oh, Val, you're so dramatic. Just be patient. Our lives will be so beautiful when we finally get together! Just a little longer." He walked closer to me and I let him near. He flashed that gorgeous smile and sang our song, "Everything I do, I do it for you." His hands grasped my arms tenderly. "You know you're the only woman I'll ever love. Trust me on this." I let him spend the night.

So I stayed silent and six months later Maggie told me he proposed. I put on the character of an excited friend, ready to assist, while inside a monsoon raged. All Eric could say to me was to be patient, and that everything would work out the way he planned.

I sat on my bed more than once holding a bottle of sleeping pills wondering how much pain I could take. I loved them both and knew Maggie would be devastated when he dropped her—just as I was devastated watching the whole drama play out.

WE LINED up in the foyer behind the closed doors, listening to the music and picturing the order in our entrance to the sanctuary, waiting for our cue to begin the procession. I turned and looked at Maggie, wanting one more chance to try to explain the seriousness of what was about to happen. My mouth could only open and close with no sound, so I hugged her instead. What a train wreck we were about to walk into, a total disaster, and I was the worst friend a person could ever have. Maybe I should have taken those sleeping pills and ended this.

"Faithful and True," the traditional bridal procession music began to play and the doors opened. One by one the bride's maids entered the giant room and slowly glided up the aisle to the front of the building to stand opposite from the groomsmen and Eric. I watched every single one of them and they moved with precision to the count of the music. My turn came and I crossed the threshold. I looked Eric directly in the eye as I walked and tried to send him mental messages to make this stop, but I suppose his receptors had tuned me out. My hands were trembling. Tears were running down my face but I kept my smile firmly smiling.

I HAD HELPED her make plans, choose colors, choose a menu and music; she and I, her mother, and the other attendants kept the appointments for fittings with the boutique for the gowns. We planned a little get-together at Maggie's mother's house for all the bridal party and families to meet and get to know each other, and Maggie "introduced me" to Eric. Pretending to be strangers, he shook my hand and I shook his, but I couldn't look at his face.

"Glad to meet you," he said to me with a slight smile in his voice.

"Nice to meet you too," was all I could manage to answer back.

"So you're Maggie's best friend? She talks about you all the time."

"Yeah, she talks about you a lot too." He sort of chuckled at me and I tried to smile back but found a desert had formed in my mouth. "Excuse me; I need to get something to drink."

Trying not to look at them together, I walked to the drinks table, but the effort of not looking was like driving by a car wreck and trying not to look at all the damage. I peeked just in time to see him lean over and kiss her on the cheek. A voice in my head screamed and I knew I was going to be sick. I ran into the house looking for the bathroom.

I found Maggie and Eric after that and told them I was ill and needed to go home and she understood. "I've heard there's a virus going around," she said. "Go home and get some rest."

"Yeah," I said. "It's a killer virus."

Another sleepless night holding the bottle of pills in my hand. How could he do this to me? I loved him so much and he couldn't see how hurt I was! He laughed at me like I was a pathetic little dog, running behind him with a stick in my mouth. Please, just throw the stick one more time.

No more. No more would I run after him. The time had come to talk to Maggie and get rid of the guilt and pain. She was my friend and she would understand. She loved me, I knew it. I was just going to get my courage together and tell her the whole story, from the adulterous adventure to the tragedy it had become. She had to know that he was planning on taking her money and leaving her for me.

Putting a single pill in my mouth, I put the bottle in the drawer beside my bed. Time was long and drawn out, but the pill finally closed my eyes and I had no dreams.

THE CHILDREN ENTERED the room and made their way to the front. Becky, Eric's four-year-old daughter, dropped the flower petals while trying extra hard to walk the "wedding walk" to the front of the room. Her little champagne colored dress sparkled as she walked and I thought about the innocence of being a little girl again. That's what I wanted to do. I wanted to go back to being a little girl and playing dress up and dolls. I wanted to hate boys again and have tea parties and play make-believe, but there was no way to get those days back. I had lost my innocence to a man who was horrible. He had tainted me, and poor Maggie would soon be just as tainted as I was.

The minister instructed everyone to stand for the bride, and the music paused, and then struck with a strong beat. Eric had his back to the minister so he could have the first glance at her. When she walked through the doors, there was a gasp, just like in a Cinderella movie. She was beautiful with her red hair swept up on her head, little tendrils of red wisps floating around her face. The pearls around her neck glowed as brightly as the beads and sequins sewn to her gown. The rest of us were insignificant little bugs next to Maggie that day, as we should have been.

My tears fell harder and my smile quivered. It should have been me. Eric should have been marrying me and I should have been the beauty walking down the aisle to meet him! The pain would be with me for the rest of my life.

THE MORNING after the engagement party I had called Maggie.

"We need to meet for lunch. There's something I need to talk to you about." We made the arrangements of where we wanted to meet and I hung up, showered, dressed and went to work. But the office was a madhouse and that day I ended up canceling lunch, telling her the "important thing" I needed to discuss was the wedding shoes and how they should be open-toed. Eric's horrible plan would stay tucked away a little longer.

The days continued on, and so did my secret pain and frustration. I began to forget things, important things, and my prized organizational skills were falling apart. I lost an entire project that had taken weeks to put together. My concentration also disappeared because all I could think of was stopping the wedding.

Eric—he was the stick that kept the pot stirred. He wouldn't leave me alone, and he wouldn't break it off with Maggie. He was the rotten thing Maggie and I had in common—the vampire feeding off my soul, and would soon destroy hers as well—but I just couldn't stop longing for him. He was an addiction that was killing me, but I couldn't let it go. I loved him, but I hated him. Our relationship would never be the same, but I died each time I thought about ending it.

SHE REACHED the front of the room and the minister asked the traditional question of who was giving this woman away. Her step-father answered, then placed her hand in Eric's and took his seat next to Maggie's mother and father and step-mother. The moment was nearing and I hoped my nerve would hold out.

The minister said a few words, then he asked the question I was waiting for.

"Is there anyone here who has a reason that these two should not be joined? Speak now, or forever hold your peace."

Complete silence. I was watching the whole thing as if it were a movie on a giant screen and I was in the balcony. I moved a few paces from Maggie and there was a loud popping sound. Eric fell at Maggie's feet and she screamed while the odor of gunpowder filled the room. There were more screams, but I couldn't tell where they came from. One of the groomsmen ran and knelt next to Eric to see why he was on the floor while a circle of red spread under his back. A splatter of red sprayed across her white gown.

I trembled so hard I could barely stand and I realized I was the other screamer. Several of the flowers in my bouquet had disintegrated when the bullet passed through them and the smoke from my gun still spilled out into the beautiful church.

I looked at Maggie and said, "I just had to make it stop."

7. SATURDAY: IN THE MOMENT

Our lips touch, lightly at first, then solidly. I feel all the breath leave my lungs with his kiss as his tongue enters my mouth, tapping my teeth as if they are a keyboard. A feeling of dizziness fogs my head and my teeth part to let the sweet-tasting muscle in. I don't remember what life was before this moment, and I'm sure there will be no life when it is over. And I don't want it to ever end. I greet his tongue with my own ballet of lust.

His hands travel gently over my body; my own hands locked tightly behind his head. He breaks the seal between our lips and his tongue glides to my cheek. His hands have left my body and now hold my face between them. Sucking in a quick breath, I am unable to open my eyes. I feel his mouth tasting me from my cheek down to my neck. Not even his teeth piercing my skin can break the spell of this moment.

His tongue laps at the blood spilling down my neck as I feel my life flow into his throat.

ABOUT THE AUTHOR

Nandy Ekle is the multi-published author of thrillers with a twist.

Her work includes stories in the following publications:

Choose or Die
Flashes in the Dark
Stitched Up
Tales of a Woman Scorned
A Pint of Bloody Fiction
Best of House of Horror
Mausoleum Memoirs
Arkham Tales

www.nandyekle.com